Murphy's Ticket

THE GOOFY START AND GLORIOUS END
OF THE CHICAGO CUBS BILLY GOAT CURSE

BRAD HERZOG AND ILLUSTRATED BY DAVID LEONARD

PUBLISHED BY SLEEPING BEAR PRESS

To my superfan sister, Laura, who has watched the Cubbies
play more games in more places than anyone I know.
The hope, passion, and loyalty in this story are reflections of hers.

—Brad

For mom and dad, who always encouraged me to draw.

—David

Sleeping Bear Press™

2395 South Huron Parkway, Suite 200, Ann Arbor, MI 48104
www.sleepingbearpress.com
© Sleeping Bear Press

Printed and bound in the United States.
10 9 8 7 6 5 4 3 2 1

Library of Congress Cataloging-in-Publication Data
Names: Herzog, Brad, author. | Leonard, David, 1979- illustrator.
Title: Murphy's ticket : the goofy start and glorious end of the Chicago Cubs
billy goat curse / written by Brad Herzog ; illustrated by David Leonard.
Description: Ann Arbor, MI : Sleeping Bear Press, [2017]
Identifiers: LCCN 2017006104 | ISBN 9781585363872
Subjects: LCSH: Chicago Cubs (Baseball team)—History—Juvenile literature.
Classification: LCC GV875.C6 H47 2017 | DDC 796.357/640977311—dc23
LC record available at https://lccn.loc.gov/2017006104

Like the famous ivy in Wrigley Field
that clings to the outfield wall,
a legend has grown throughout the years
about the curse of Chicago baseball.

It tells of a goat who lived long ago
and the fans of a lovable team,
who never lost their loyalty
or their faith in a World Series dream.

The story began with a bump in the road,
and that goat in the back of a truck.
Who would believe that this was the start
of Chicago Cubs baseball bad luck?

As the baby goat stood on his spindly legs,
over the bump the truck rumbled.
The goat lost his footing, flew head over hooves,
and right out the back he then tumbled.

So the curious fellow wandered the city,
staring up at all the skyscrapers.
He kicked some stray cans, chased them around,
and nibbled on daily newspapers.

At that time, a fellow named Billy Sianis
owned a Chicago saloon.
He needed more customers. Business was slow.
He tried everything under the moon.

What else can I do? Billy wondered,
keeping busy by sweeping the floor.
Suddenly a bright light filled the room,
and a little goat skipped through the door.

Billy looked down at his furry, young guest,
and he knew the moment they met
that their paths had crossed for a reason.
He hugged this lost goat—a new pet!

"I'll call you Murphy," Billy announced.
"You'll have a new home here. Why not?"
And soon it was rare to see Billy without
his long-eared, four-legged mascot.

His customers soon loved Murphy, too,
and Billy Sianis took note.
He shaved his beard into a goatee
and said, "Just call me Billy Goat!"

That's how the Billy Goat Tavern was born.
But how did it rise to great fame?
Well, Billy Goat purchased two tickets
to a fateful World Series game.

It was October 6, 1945,
and even on that long-ago date,
the Cubs hadn't won a championship
since way back in 1908.

Yet the loyal fans packed Wrigley Field
for a World Series played in the sun.
The outlook was brilliant for the home team.
They led Detroit two games to one.

And who came to root for the Cubs that fine day?
Billy Goat and his faithful sidekick.
One ticket for him, and one for his pal,
although Murphy just gave it a lick.

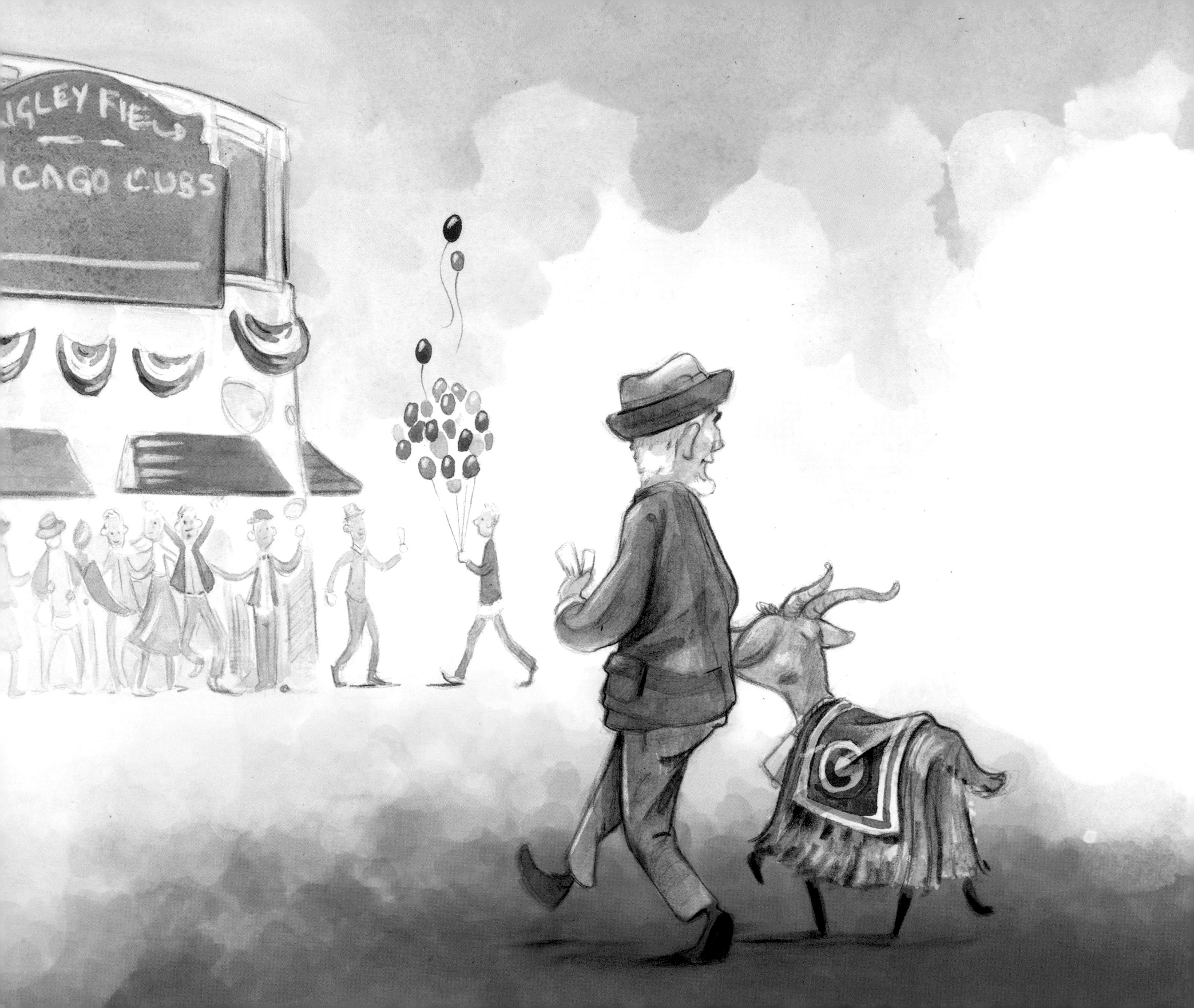

IGLEY FIEL
ICAGO CUBS

As Billy marched right into Wrigley,
Murphy trotted close behind.
The pair paraded around the field,
and at first no one seemed to mind.

The spectators cheered this strange new Cubs fan.
Murphy bucked and galloped with pride.
And that outfield grass? It looked delicious!
The little goat's eyes opened wide.

When the game was about to begin,
Billy said, "It's time to get seated.
Come on, Murphy! It's the World Series!"
"Meh," was all the goat bleated.

A man was supposed to seat them,
but instead he just blocked their path.
"No chance," he said. "That goat really stinks."
It was true. Murphy needed a bath.

"Billy Goat, you can stay," said the man,
"but Murphy, well, he has to go."
Billy stood quietly, let out a sigh,
and then whispered a single word. "No."

Sure, Billy loved the Cubbies,
but he loved Murphy most of all.
Nothing meant more to him than his dear pet.
Not even World Series baseball.

Maybe the sky grew suddenly dark;
clouds blew in on that sunny day.
Maybe time stopped, just for a moment.
What now would Billy Goat say?

Billy peered toward the big, wooden scoreboard.
His cheeks and his eyes became red.
"Them Cubs, they ain't gonna win no more!"
are the fateful words Billy Goat said.

He stomped straight out of the ballpark,
muttering "Those Cubbies, they're done!"
And so began years of Cubs misery.
Billy Goat's Curse had begun.

The Cubbies lost that ball game,
and they dropped the next one, as well.
In fact, when they lost the World Series,
Billy Goat asked, "Now who smells?"

"Wait 'til next year!" Cubs fans declared.
And they really believed every word.
But once the next season was over,
the Cubbies found themselves in third.

The following year, the Cubs came in sixth.
Their fortunes had fallen so fast.
The year after that, they lost 90 games.
The Cubbies finished in last.

As the years passed, the spirit of Murphy
seemed to visit the Cubs now and then.
Whenever it seemed that the team would come close,
the curse would just pop up again.

He was there when a black cat ran onto the field,
surely an unlucky sign,
and the Cubs suddenly dropped from first place
in late summer 1969.

When a ball rolled through the first baseman's legs
in the playoffs, 1984,
and the Cubs missed out on the World Series again,
had Murphy been watching the score?

In 2003, in the playoffs again,
history was in the making.
Cubs fans believed it might be the year.
The stadium seemed to be shaking.

With just one more win, they'd reach the World Series.
Chicago led in the eighth inning.
A pop-up was hit. The crowd held its breath.
The Cubs were just five outs from winning.

But some fans got in the way that day.
The left fielder couldn't catch the foul ball.
Eight runs scored. Murphy could not be ignored
after this, the closest near miss of all.

Every time the Cubbies fell short,
breaking each loyal fan's heart,
lots of them wondered, Is Murphy still here?
Is that goat still playing a part?

The Cubs, those Lovable Losers,
tried so many ways to reverse
that strangeness that had made them suffer so long,
known simply as Billy Goat's Curse.

They sprayed holy water, blew up that foul ball,
and brought goats to Opening Day.
Yet always the Cubs just found new ways to lose.
Murphy would not go away.

But 2016? It felt different.
The Cubs were baseball's best team.
After so many frustrating seasons,
Chicago fans still dared to dream.

Go count a baseball's red stitches.
You'll find one hundred and eight,
the same number of years since the Cubbies were champs.
Hey hey! Holy cow! Was it fate?

And then on a crisp autumn night
at the field on Chicago's North Side,
the Cubs FINALLY won the National League!
A whole city swelled with great pride.

Could they really win the World Series?
Cleveland's team would be their foe.
Down three games to one, the Cubs needed to win
each of the three games to go.

The Cubs won Game 5 and then Game 6, too.
One final night would decide it.
With four outs to go, Chicago was winning!
But wouldn't you know, Cleveland tied it.

Cubs fans all over the country
thought back to the curse and their pain.
And that's when the clouds began weeping.
That's right. It started to rain.

Was it the tears from so many years?
From so many Cubs fans in the sky
who had never been able to witness
a World Series "**W**" fly?

But then the rain suddenly stopped.
After midnight, the Cubs grabbed their bats.
And in the tenth inning, the Cubs won the game!
No more curse! No foul balls! No black cats!

Fans in Chicago poured into the streets!
The Cubs were the kings of baseball!
And it might be—it could be—that somewhere,
Murphy cheered loudest of all.

Do you believe in Billy Goat's Curse? If not, consider this:

In 1969, the Cubs were in first place for 155 days. But they lost 17 out of their last 25 games and finished in second place behind New York's "Miracle Mets." The general manager and the announcer for the Mets had the same last name: MURPHY.

In 1984, the Cubs reached the playoffs for the first time in 39 years. They won their first two games against the San Diego Padres, but they lost the last three at San Diego's ballpark—Jack MURPHY Stadium.

In 2015, the Cubs made it to the National League Championship Series, but the Mets beat them, thanks to a batting hero who slugged four home runs. His name? Daniel MURPHY.

When the Cubs beat the Los Angeles Dodgers to finally return to the World Series, the date was October 22, 2016—exactly 46 years to the day after "Billy Goat" Sianis passed away.